Here Comes Santa Claus

Text copyright © 1947, 1970 by Gene Autry Music Publishing, Inc.

Copyright assigned 1948 to Western Music Publishing Co.

Illustrations copyright © 2002 by Bruce Whatley

Printed in the U.S.A. All rights reserved.

www.harperchildrens.com

Library of Congress Cataloging-in-Publication Data

Autry, Gene, 1907–

Here comes Santa Claus / words and music by Gene Autry and Oakley Haldeman ;
illustrated by Bruce Whatley.

p.   cm.

Summary: Santa Claus is riding down Santa Claus Lane tonight with toys for all
girls and boys.

ISBN 0-06-028268-1 — ISBN 0-06-028269-X (lib. bdg.)

1. Christmas music—Texts. 2. Children's songs—Texts. [1. Santa Claus—Songs
and music. 2. Christmas music. 3. Songs.] I. Haldeman, Oakley, 1911–
II. Whatley, Bruce, ill. III. Title.

PZ8.3.A9375 He 2002

782.42'1723'0268—dc21                                                    2001039373

[E]                                                                            CIP

                                                                                AC

Typography by Al Cetta      1 2 3 4 5 6 7 8 9 10      ❖      First Edition

# Here Comes Santa Claus

WORDS AND MUSIC

BY GENE AUTRY
AND OAKLEY HALDEMAN

ILLUSTRATED BY

BRUCE WHATLEY

HARPERCOLLINSPUBLISHERS

Here comes Santa Claus! Here comes Santa Claus!
Right down Santa Claus Lane!
Vixen and Blitzen and all his reindeer
Are pulling on the rein.

Bells are ringing, children singing,
All is merry and bright.

Hang your stockings and say your prayers,
'Cause Santa Claus comes tonight.

Here comes Santa Claus! Here comes Santa Claus!
Right down Santa Claus Lane!
He's got a bag that is filled with toys
For the boys and girls again.

Hear those sleigh bells jingle jangle,
What a beautiful sight.

Jump in bed, cover up your head,
'Cause Santa Claus comes tonight.

Here comes Santa Claus! Here comes Santa Claus!
Right down Santa Claus Lane!
He doesn't care if you're rich or poor
For he loves you just the same.

Santa knows that we're God's children—
That makes everything right.

Fill your hearts with a Christmas cheer,
'Cause Santa Claus comes tonight.

Here comes Santa Claus! Here comes Santa Claus!
Right down Santa Claus Lane!
He'll come around when the chimes ring out—
Then it's Christmas morn again.

Peace on Earth will come to all
If we just follow the light.

Dear Matthew
This is Tinsel. She is a
very special puppy.
Give her loving care.
Merry Christmas
Santa

Let's give thanks to the Lord above,
'Cause Santa Claus comes tonight!

# Here Comes Santa Claus

## (Right Down Santa Claus Lane)

Words and Music by
GENE AUTRY
and OAKLEY HALDEMAN

Here comes Sant-a Claus! Here comes Sant-a Claus! Right down Sant-a Claus Lane!

Vix - en and Blitz - en and all his rein - deer Are pull - ing on the rein.
He's got a bag that is filled with toys For the boys and girls a - gain.
He does - n't care if you're rich or poor For he loves you just the same.
He'll come a - round when the chimes ring out— Then it's Christ - mas morn a - gain.